HALFDAN RASMUSSEN

(1915–2002)
One of Denmark's best-loved poets.
This book is dedicated to his
memory, and to his daughter,
Iben Nagel Rasmussen.

—M. N.

First U.S. edition 2006

Library of Congress Cataloging-in-Publication
Data is available.
Library of Congress Catalog Card Number
2004062940
ISBN 0-7636-2282-6

10 9 8 7 6 5 4 3 2 1
Printed in China

This book was typeset in Officina Serif.
The illustrations were done in acrylic.

Candlewick Press
2067 Massachusetts Avenue
Cambridge, Massachusetts 02140

visit us at www.candlewick.com

Halfdan Rasmussen

THE LADDER

TRANSLATED BY

Marilyn Nelson

ILLUSTRATED BY

Pierre Pratt

CANDLEWICK PRESS
CAMBRIDGE, MASSACHUSETTS

A ladder that was fine and young
with fresh red paint on every rung
was taken to a lonely lane,
where, long forgotten, it remained.

The carpenter who'd built the ladder
and who was always very matter-
of-fact had climbed it with a grin
and never climbed back down again.

For when he'd reached the ladder's top,
he'd just decided not to stop
and done a disappearing act
into thin air, as a matter of fact.

The ladder stood around awhile

acting bored (in ladder style)

and wondering rather idly why

LIFT

the carpenter was in the sky.

Then it thought that it would be
remarkable to go and see
what's in the great wide world out there
to see, if you go anywhere.

So first it did a little dance,

then it did a little prance,

then, as nicely as you please,

it waddled off with stiff red knees.

It met a large brown animal
and thought, Oh, how unusual:
two horns, four legs, a swishing tail,
and a rope that's tied up to a rail!

The ladder asked it, "Who are you?
A mouse? A house? Oh, tell me, do!"
The cow the ladder said this to
stared blankly back and answered,

"Moo!"

The ladder wandered off again,
a tall, thin, red pedestrian,
and walked until it ascertained
it was walking on a dead-end lane.

Then it stopped and looked agog
at a farmer wearing wooden clogs,
who smoked his pipe and tapped his toe
and very calmly said, "Hello."

On his head he had a hat.
On his arm he had a cat.
That's all there is about the cat—

it ran away and that was that.

The farmer didn't seem surprised
but climbed, instead, into the sky.
And when he reached the ladder's top,
he entered heaven with a hop.

So the ladder waited there,
taking in the pleasant air,
then, since it had some time to kill,
it waddled slowly down the hill.

The day was fine, for it was June.
The ladder heard a lively tune
and saw, far off, a marching band
led by a high-stepping man.

The band marched, keeping perfect time,
with drum and horn and fife and chime.
With a root-toot-toot and a rat-tat-tatter,
they marched right to the foot of the ladder.

The pretty ladder heaved a sigh
under the clear and brilliant sky
and thought about the marching band,
whose music had been really grand.

And from the distant cloudless blue
came a rat-tat-tat and roo-too-too
from the musicians who had gone
to heaven playing marching songs.

While the ladder stood and dreamed,
a car raced up whose tires screamed,
whose horn beep-beeped, whose motor roared,
whose owner had his own chauffeur.

The band marched smartly to the tunes
played by tubas and bassoons.
They marched right up into the air
and disappeared with a great fanfare!

LIFT

LIFT ▶

Its brakes squealed, but it didn't stop
when it reached the ladder's top.
Instead it drove into the air
and left the ladder standing there.

It stood there for an hour or so,
until it felt the urge to go,
for it had better things to do
than looking up into the blue.

But just as it prepared to stalk
off to take another walk,
a mouse ran toward it through the daisies,
chased by a cat that mewed like crazy.

A black dog, which was rather fat,
pursued the swiftly running cat,
which chased the mouse, which fled in fright,
squeaking loudly in its flight.

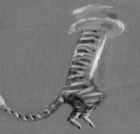

Since they could not stop to think,
they reached the ladder in a wink
and ran into the sky, all three,
with open mouth and straightened knee.

The ladder by this time was sweating
from the excitement it was getting.
It's difficult to walk all day
when people climb on you that way.

It stood and looked the meadow over
and then it saw a pair of lovers:
a lovely girl who held the hand
of a beautiful young man.

They walked and dreamed, this loving pair,
with summer flowers in their hair,
and as they walked, they seemed to hear
sweet music from the stratosphere.

The ladder rested for a while.

They ascended, cheek to cheek,
so much in love they couldn't speak,
and entered heaven wearing smiles.

Then it thought,

What can this be?

There must be something wrong with me.

This isn't normal. I must stop

folks from jumping off my top!

I guess I should be heading home.
Ladders probably shouldn't roam.

Besides, the sky was blue all day,
but now it's looking thunder gray.

Suddenly a lightning bolt   hit the ladder with a jolt,

knocking it into a tizzy

and making it extremely dizzy.

The lightning stood there a whole minute

in the sky with dark clouds in it,

and looked exactly like a stair

descending from the storm up there.

And down the lightning at a jog
came the farmer wearing clogs,

and
the
band
marched
d
o
w
n
in
rhythm,

and the lovers, too, descended,
whose sweet music never ended,

and the long-lost carpenter
whom we heard of long before
took his ladder on the train,
and he has not been seen again.